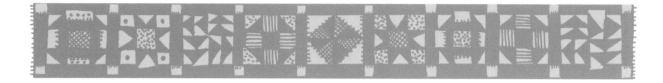

THE
OLD AFRICAN

Julius Lester

Illustrated by Jerry Pinkney

DIAL BOOKS

DIAL BOOKS
A member of Penguin Group (USA) Inc.
Published by The Penguin Group
Penguin Group (USA) Inc., 375 Hudson Street, New York, NY 10014, U.S.A.
Penguin Group (Canada), 10 Alcorn Avenue, Toronto, Ontario, Canada M4V 3B2
(a division of Pearson Penguin Canada Inc.)
Penguin Books Ltd, 80 Strand, London WC2R 0RL, England
Penguin Ireland, 25 St. Stephen's Green, Dublin 2, Ireland (a division of Penguin Books Ltd)
Penguin Group (Australia), 250 Camberwell Road, Camberwell, Victoria 3124, Australia
(a division of Pearson Australia Group Pty Ltd)
Penguin Books India Pvt Ltd, 11 Community Centre, Panchsheel Park, New Delhi - 110 017, India
Penguin Group (NZ), Cnr Airborne and Rosedale Roads, Albany, Auckland 1310, New Zealand
(a division of Pearson New Zealand Ltd)
Penguin Books (South Africa) (Pty) Ltd, 24 Sturdee Avenue, Rosebank, Johannesburg
2196, South Africa
Penguin Books Ltd, Registered Offices: 80 Strand, London WC2R 0RL, England

Text copyright © 2005 by Julius Lester
Illustrations copyright © 2005 by Jerry Pinkney
All rights reserved
Designed by Jerry Pinkney with Atha Tehon
Text set in Goudy Newstyle
Manufactured in China on acid-free paper
1 3 5 7 9 10 8 6 4 2

Library of Congress Cataloging-in-Publication Data
Lester, Julius.
The Old African / Julius Lester ; illustrated by Jerry Pinkney.
p. cm.
Summary: An elderly slave uses the power of his mind to ease the
suffering of his fellow slaves and eventually lead them back to Africa.
Based on an actual incident from black history.
ISBN 0-8037-2564-7
[1. Slavery—Fiction. 2. African Americans—Fiction.
3. Extrasensory perception—Fiction. 4. Telepathy—Fiction.]
I. Pinkney, Jerry, ill. II. Title.
PZ7.L56290l 2005 [Fic]—dc22 2003015671

The full-color artwork was prepared using graphite, gouache, pastel,
and watercolor on paper.

Please note: Although based on an actual incident from black history,
this is a work of the imagination.

To **Donna Riley** *and*
my wife, **Milan,**
for being there when I went
into the hold of the ship
J.L.

To the spirit of the **Ybo** *peoples*
and all those who to this day
resist the yoke of slavery
J.P.

I

The boy's wrists were tied so that his arms hugged the trunk of the large oak tree. His face was pressed against it as if it were the bosom of the mother he had never known. His back glistened red with blood.

Whack!

The whip cut into his flesh again, but he did not scream or even whimper.

Master Riley had ordered his twenty slaves to watch what happened to someone who dared run away, and like a black crescent moon, they stood in a semicircle near the tree. At the center was the Old African. His face was as expressionless as tree bark.

The slaves did not see the blood on the boy's back nor hear the flies droning around the red gaping wounds. They were staring at a picture in their minds, a picture of water as soft and cool as a lullaby. They did not know how the Old African was able to make them see water as blue as freedom, but he had done it to them often.

Anytime there was pain among them, be it from childbirth or a whipping, the Old African took over their minds and made them into one mind that saw and felt the same thing. They could feel him taking their pictures of the water's cool wetness and putting them into the mind of the boy to stop the burning heat of his pain. That was why the boy had not screamed or even cried, though blood lay thick on his back.

"You have the power." That was what the Old African's father had told him when he was a boy, had told him before he was taken across the Water-That-Stretched-Forever and brought here, had told him before he became the Old African. He was Jaja then. God's gift. No one here knew his name. All of them, even Master Riley, said he had been born old, had been born old-looking, though he wasn't, not if you counted birthdays.

Obasi had told him he was as old as air. Obasi was the elder who had taught him how to change into an eagle, a crocodile, a snake, a tree, a flower, or a stone. But those were merely tricks. More difficult had been learning how to catch the tears of another before they fell, how to hold the hurting in a heart so it would not break, how to keep the living alive—and the dead too.

Whack!

As the whip tore yet more skin from the boy's back, exposing the raw, red, bloody meat of his flesh, a shaft of searing pain struck the Old African in the chest as the boy cried out for the first time. The Old African almost staggered from the intensity of it, but quickly focused his energy and pushed the pain down into his abdomen, through his legs and feet and into the earth.

Fear, anger, and sorrow were beginning to enter the feelings and minds of the slaves. The Old African knew he was not going to be able to keep their minds fixed on water much longer. Without their minds he could not protect the boy from such great pain.

The Old African could have known any of their most secret thoughts. Sometimes he spoke to them in their minds, though his lips never moved. But no one had ever heard his voice in all the years he had been on the plantation—not even May, who talked to him almost every day and was standing beside him now.

The Old African had trained himself not to eavesdrop on the souls of others merely to satisfy his curiosity. But when any of them were in pain, he slipped inside their souls as effortlessly and quietly as a bird going from a tree to the ground, and pulled the pain from the channels of their souls as if it were a worm in the earth. Sometimes, however, like now, the pain was too great for him alone and he needed their minds. But they had not been trained since childhood to focus on a single object for hours without letting their minds and feelings tremble as much as a leaf when a bird alit on a twig.

Whack!

The boy cried out louder and the Old African felt waves of pain as high and stony as mountains. He had not known such pain since the journey across the Water-That-Stretched-Forever. If Riley did not stop soon, the boy would die.

As if sensing this also, or perhaps the Old African put the thought in his mind, Riley suddenly handed the whip to William, the slave who drove his buggy and took care of the horses. "Clean the blood off and put some fat on it. That's my best whip. I don't want it to crack from blood drying on it."

"Yah, suh," William responded, rolling the whip up and going off toward the stable.

Riley turned and faced the slaves, his hands on his hips, the heels resting lightly on the hilt of a knife in a scabbard on one side and the handle of a pistol in a holster on the other. "I ought to kill that nigger, but I won't. He ain't the first one of y'all what run away, and you know me. I don't get upset if one of y'all wants to sneak off to see your wife or husband or one of your children what live on a nearby plantation.

"Hell, I'd probably do the same. But I ain't got no tolerance for a nigger what runs off and don't plan on coming back. It took me two weeks to find this nigger, and when I found him, he was down by the ocean! That's right! If any one of you tries a stunt like that, I will beat you to death! You understand me? I will kill you just as sure as my name is John Riley!"

The Old African waited impatiently for Riley to shut up. The boy's heart was fluttering desperately, like the wings of a bird caught in a trap.

"You all go on back to work now. But Paul has to stay tied to that tree 'til morning. I want him to feel the mosquitoes sucking on him all night and I want y'all to go to sleep hearing him moan and cry. I'm a good man, but this is what happens when you push me too far."

The boy's heartbeat was so faint now that the Old African dared not wait any longer. He went quickly over to the tree and without hesitating, May followed. Quickly they untied the boy's wrists and he slumped unconscious into May's arms. The Old African put his right hand over the boy's heart and pressed down firmly. Immediately he felt a warmth flowing from his heart, through his arm, and down into the boy's heart. After a moment it began beating with a stronger and more steady rhythm.

"What the hell do you think you're doing?" Riley yelled at the Old African. "Are you deaf? I said to leave him tied up until morning!" Riley's upper lip curled into a sneer and his eyes lusted with the desire to shed more blood. He jerked the pistol from its holster.

The Old African turned his head and stared at Riley. Obasi had taught him how to look at a man and cover his mind so that he forgot what he was supposed to be doing, to look at a man and make it impossible for him to move, to look at a man and squeeze the blood from his heart, causing him to die where he stood.

But Obasi had also taught him that just because he had a power, it did not mean he was supposed to use it.

The Old African focused his gaze on a place between and slightly above Riley's eyes. Obasi had called it the Place of True Seeing. If you knew how to look into it, you could see the color of a person's soul and read his thoughts as if they were words on a page.

Riley's finger tightened on the pistol's trigger. Suddenly he heard a voice: "Put away your pistol or I will kill you where you stand."

Riley was looking at the Old African, but his lips had not moved. "Who said that?" Riley yelled, his voice trembling as he spun around to look at the slaves. "Dammit! Who said that?"

The slaves stared at him. They had not heard anything.

"Who said that?" he repeated, looking back at the Old African. But the Old African had turned his back to the slave owner and was picking the boy up.

"I did," the voice said. "Here. Over here."

Riley turned toward the sound of the voice and found himself staring at the oak tree to which the boy had been tied.

"Put away your pistol!"

Riley's eyes grew large. "That's impossible!" he said to the tree.

"Not at all," the tree responded.

Riley began trembling visibly. The Old African was the one doing all this . . . all this—whatever it was. Trickery! Voodoo! Riley was sorry he had ever bought him. He had tried to sell him many times, but who would buy a slave who never spoke a word and looked like he would kill you in your sleep as easily as you killed a mosquito. Well, John Riley was not going to wait around for that black son of a bitch to work some hoodoo on him! If there was any dying to be done on the Riley plantation, that bastard was going to do it. Riley tried to turn and fire the pistol at the back of the Old African as he carried the boy to the cabin in the woods where he lived apart from the other slaves.

But Riley's arms were as heavy as stones and he could not turn his body. Suddenly, the pistol dropped from his hand and he stumbled over his feet and almost fell as he ran to get away, ran to the house where he would drink bourbon until he passed out. He did not know that the Old African would know the exact instant he passed into unconsciousness.

II

For two days and nights the Old African stayed awake to put herbs on the boy's wounds and brew teas for him to drink. The rest of the time he held the boy's soul in his hands as if it were a baby and told it to stay in this world awhile longer. It would have helped if he had known the boy's true name. Paul was no kind of name. The boy needed a name like Kantigi, a faithful person—or Chinua, God's own blessing. It was hard to save a soul if you did not know its name. But he had known the name to which the soul of Ola, his wife, answered. However, the knowing had not kept her soul from retreating when warriors of another tribe attacked their village in the middle of the night.

It happened so quickly. One minute he had been asleep, one arm across Ola's back. The next there were screams and yells and shouts, and then men bursting into his home and grabbing him and Ola, tying their hands behind their backs and pushing them outside.

Quickly he was separated from Ola. A rope was tied around his waist and then tied to the bound wrists of a man in front of him as his own bound wrists were tied to a rope around the waist of the man behind him.

"Ola! Ola!"

"Jaja! Jaja!" Her cry came from somewhere in the darkness.

He looked for his parents, but it was impossible to see anyone clearly in the darkness. When dawn came, he saw that about forty of them had been caught, mostly men. However, Jaja was happy when he saw that he was tied to Obasi!

"What is going on? What is happening to us?"

Obasi shook his head. "I do not know, Jaja." There was sadness and fear in his voice, notes Jaja had never heard from the music of Obasi's soul.

It was light enough now for Jaja to see his wife a short distance away. "Ola! Ola!"

Her face showed no joy at seeing him. She motioned with her head and he followed her gaze and saw four bodies on the ground, one of whom he recognized as her father!

"*Ayyyyyy!*" he cried out as much over his inability to hold her as in anguish for the murdered ones.

He looked around again for his parents, but did not see them. Perhaps they had escaped into the forest, as it seemed most of the people in the village had. But as he turned to look once more at the bodies, the one lying next to Ola's father could have been that of his own. Forgetting that he was tied, he took a step toward the bodies only to be stopped by the ropes at his waist and wrists and by the shouts of all the others who stumbled when he moved so abruptly.

"I think that is my father!" he called out to those shouting at him. "My father!"

"Shut up!" a harsh voice told him as he simultaneously felt the hard, cold point of a spear at his abdomen.

"Let's get out of here," another voice called, and the captives were pushed forward.

They were marched for three days through the forest. Jaja did not recognize what tribe his captors belonged to or understand their tongue, though several of them spoke enough of his to make themselves understood. And whenever he asked where they were being taken, the captors responded with a laughter that bristled with the hostility of secrets not shared.

The men and women were kept separate and Jaja could only look at Ola, her skin as softly black as a crow's flight. They had known each other since they were children, had always known they would marry, had known they would have each other for as long as there were stars. He tried to use the power to push away the fear he saw in her eyes. If he did not do something, the fear would eventually trickle into her spirit and take her away from him. But he was only nineteen, too young to know how to save her spirit, especially when he had to tend his own.

Shortly after they began marching again on the third day, there came a noise unlike any Jaja had ever heard. It had no beginning, middle, or end, no high tone or low, just a constant and unchanging roar like some beast that never had to pause for breath.

"What is that?" they asked their captors and each other.

Their captors laughed a laugh that did not bring smiles to anyone's lips, not even their own.

As they got closer, the roaring became louder and louder. Finally, Jaja recognized it as the sound of rushing water, but he could not imagine a river so large that its sound would fill the sky.

Before too much longer, the path through the palm and coconut trees ended and the captured ones emerged from the forest into a bright and harsh sunlight against which they had to close their eyes. The earth had changed from the dark hardness of the forest floor to a hot, loose whiteness beneath their feet, which moved and slid with every step they took, spurting between their toes. They stumbled and staggered as they tried to maintain their balance.

As their eyes adjusted to the glaring light, they saw what had been making the roaring noise, a noise now so loud, they could scarcely hear each other's voices, if anyone had known what to say. This was no river, but Jaja did not have a word for water that stretched until it touched the sky at the edge of the world, but here, closest to him, it reared up like it wanted to swallow the earth. How could there be so much water? And why was it so angry?

Then Jaja noticed farther out, where the water did not seem as angry, a large and oddly-shaped house. Was that where they were going to be taken? Who lived there? Why would someone live in a house on the water? Fear seized the captured ones anew and everyone talked at once, though no one could hear another. But terror was easily understood.

Jaja saw a group of men walking toward them, perhaps ten or fifteen. Their skin was white like sorrow. The voices of the captured ones erupted into moans and screams louder than the roar of the water.

"Mwene Puto! Mwene Puto!" came the shouts from various ones, and they tried to raise their hands and point at the white men.

Their people had stories about Mwene Puto, the Lord of the Dead, who was the color of bones. But their stories had not told them there was more than one Mwene Puto! The captured ones knew now they were going to be killed. No longer caring that they were tied to each other, they strained and pulled at their ropes, trying to escape. But their captors rushed forward and thrust spears against their bellies, looking as if nothing would make them happier than to push the spears into their flesh.

When the Lords of the Dead reached them, they talked with their captors. Jaja saw one of the lords give their captors beads, and they disappeared back into the forest. The Lords of the Dead cut the ropes from their wrists and from around their waists, and replaced them immediately with iron cuffs around their wrists, ankles, and necks. Iron chains were then fastened on, linking each one to the other by the hands and neck.

"Sit!" One Lord of the Dead surprised them by speaking in their tongue. As soon as they did, other lords came forward and ripped their clothes from their bodies.

The captured ones cried out against their nakedness. Jaja saw one of the lords pinch the now exposed nipple of a woman.

Anger filled Jaja when a lord tore off his clothing. But when the lord took the clothing off Ndulu, the man chained behind Jaja, Ndulu bit into the wrist of the lord.

The lord screamed and tried to pull away, but Ndulu would not let go, though blood from the wrist had begun trickling down his mouth and chin. Then the lord pulled a stick from his pocket and pointed it at Ndulu.

Boom!

Jaja started at the loud noise and his nose wrinkled at the acrid smell of smoke coming from the end of the stick. Then he felt himself being pulled down as Ndulu slumped to the ground, blood pouring from a hole in his head. Jaja found himself lying atop Ndulu, so close that he heard his last gasps of life.

The other captives fought to maintain their balance, but as those closest saw that one of them was dead, they began pulling backward. This provoked screams and yells as people pulled in different directions, which caused the iron cuffs to bite into their wrists and ankles.

Boom! The stick was pointed at the sky.

The captives stopped.

"Take a good look," the one who spoke their tongue said, now pointing at the figure on the ground. "This is a fire-stick! Each of us has one, and we will use our fire-sticks to kill anyone who tries to hurt us or run away. Is that understood?"

The captives nodded their heads eagerly, moaning and whimpering in fear. One of the lords unchained Jaja from the dead man, and others dragged his body to the edge of the forest and left it there. Jaja was refastened to the next man and it was as if Ndulu had never been among them. These men were truly the Lords of the Dead that they could cause a stick to make a loud sound and breathe smoke, and with that alone, kill you.

"Sit!"

When they were seated, the Lords of the Dead came among them. One held the neck of a captive while the other scraped the hair off his head with a flat piece of shiny metal. The screams were as constant now as the roar of the Water-That-Stretched-Forever and sometimes it took two Lords of the Dead to hold a captive still while his head was shaved. When Jaja's turn came, he kept his scream inside.

Finally, it was over. Their scalps burned and bled, but they felt as if more than their hair had been taken. Jaja tried to imagine how he looked with more hair beneath his arms and around his penis than on his head. He did not want to look for Ola, afraid he would not know her from any other woman, afraid she would not recognize him. However, his eyes found her. She did not look at him. Her head was bowed and her arms were crossed over her breasts as she sought to hide them from the eyes of the lords staring at the women with naked lust.

"Stand up!"

The captured ones were almost glad to have something to do, and their chains rattled as they got to their feet.

"Start walking!"

They moved stolidly down the slope toward the water, their feet more steady now on the hot white earth that shifted with their steps. Except for an occasional moan or sob, the only other sound was the roar of the Water-That-Stretched-Forever. Boats were coming toward them from the house on the water. What was going to happen now? Jaja wondered. Were they going to be taken to that house? Then what? Nothing made sense, except . . . except that the Lords of the Dead were going to eat them. What else would they want them for?

"Sit!"

As they sat down, Jaja looked to his right where the land went upward. There at its top stood a huge building of stone. Steps curved from the building to the white earth and coming down those steps were what seemed like hundreds of captives, chained to each other. As they reached the bottom of the steps, they were shoved into small boats that, when full, began moving toward the house on the water.

"Up!"

It was their time. The Lords of the Dead pushed them down to the edge of the water. The captured ones began screaming and crying as the cold water lapped at their feet. But the Lords of the Dead forced them into the boats.

The screams and cries of the captives were as relentless as the roar of the water as the small boat was rowed to the house on the water by two Lords of the Dead. When they arrived, they were pushed and prodded up steps made of rope that hung down the sides of the house. Finally all the captives had come up the ladder.

There were more Lords of the Dead in the house on the water. Some of these lords rushed forward and made the captives line up next to each other in rows, the women in front, the men behind.

Then one of the lords came toward them, a stick in his mouth from which smoke curled. Jaja waited tensely for the stick to make a loud noise and kill them, but nothing happened. Instead the lord began looking in the mouth of the woman at the end of the first row. He pulled on her teeth, squeezed her breasts, thighs, and buttocks. Minutes later Jaja felt hands squeeze his arms and thighs.

Finally the man had felt all of them and for whatever reason, seemed satisfied.

"Sit down! We're going to feed you!"

The lords gave the captives tin plates with what looked like peas mixed with cornmeal. Jaja dipped his fingers in and brought it to his mouth. That's what it was, flavored with palm oil, salt, and pepper.

As he ate, he noticed some of the lords climbing long poles. As they let out large pieces of white cloth, the captives commented to one another about how pretty the cloth was.

Suddenly, there came a loud screeching noise, and Jaja saw a large piece of iron being pulled up out of the water. The pieces of cloth puffed outward and the house began moving.

The captured ones leaped to their feet, plates of food falling to the floor. Even chained together as they were, they were like one person as they rushed to the side, where they could see the palm and coconut trees and the stone house on the hilltop moving farther and farther away. Overhead, white birds with black-tipped wings squawked loudly as if they, too, were sorry, while the screams of the captives were so loud, they could be heard on shore.

"Down below! Down below!" came a shouted command, and quickly, the captives were pushed into the bottom of the ship. Their cuffs were unlocked and some began striking their heads against the sides of the ship, moaning and screaming while others rushed to go back up the steps but were beaten back with whips.

The bottom of the ship was three tiers of wide wooden bunks, three feet between each one. The captives were made to lie on their right sides, their bodies curled against each other like spoons resting in a drawer. Jaja could feel the head of the man behind lying on his back, the man's knees resting in the crooks of Jaja's knees just as Jaja's head lay on the back of the man in front of him, his knees and thighs tucked in the crook of the other man's legs.

Jaja lay in the middle tier, which he found out quickly was the worst place to be. Even though there were round windows that brought in air from the water, and open hatches in the ceiling let in more air, it was not enough for the almost 250 men, women, and children who lay as tightly against each other as feathers on a bird's wings.

Almost immediately Jaja was covered with sweat, as was the man who lay against him, as was the man he lay against, as were the bodies of every man, woman, and child lying there. The smell of perspiration was too thick for the wisps of air coming in from the water to move against. Someone gagged at the odor and vomited. Then another. And another. And another.

The odors of sweat and vomit combined with the smell of terror and sorrow. Jaja smelled the loosening bowels nearby and then felt something wet drop onto his forehead, neck, and back from the tier above. A moment later the bowels of the man against whom he lay let go, and then, to his shame, his own. He wished he were Ndulu. Even now, so many years later, any unpleasant odor returned the Old African to the hot, wet, stinking darkness in the bottom of the ship, the sound of the waves slapping its sides, the creak of the masts and sails as the vessel keeled from one side to the other.

The next morning they were taken up on deck. Jaja squinted against the brightness of the sun to see where they were, but there was only water as wide as despair. Pails filled with water were brought, and Jaja and the others washed themselves of the excrement and urine caked on their faces and bodies like sun-baked mud.

As he cleaned himself, Jaja gazed into the sky. How could it be so beautifully blue and not know nor care that he was so miserable? He then looked longingly at the ocean and wondered if even that would be enough water to make him feel clean again. When he was done, he sat down, closed his eyes, and inhaled the air deeply. However, he was afraid that the stench had taken root in the passageways of his nostrils and nothing could ever dislodge it.

Breakfast was beans. As Jaja took the tin plate, he saw Ola a short distance away, a lord next to her, his hands rubbing her breasts, his mouth wide with laughter. Jaja moved toward them immediately, but his path was blocked by Obasi.

"Get out of my way!" Jaja told him.

"I cannot," Obasi whispered. "You must not!"

"I know what he is going to do to Ola. She needs me!"

"Your people need you too, Jaja. They will need you more than ever now. You are the only one who has the power."

"But you have the power too."

Obasi shook his head. "My power has grown weak and is no match for such cruelty as this. Listen to me, Jaja. My spirit is leaving me. I am not going to survive this. You must."

Jaja shook his head. "I do not want to, my teacher! I do not want to!"

Obasi nodded. "I understand. But if you die, they too will die. Oh, not in their bodies. But here." He put his hand gently over his heart.

Suddenly there came a loud yell of pain. The lord who had been touching Ola was grasping his neck and when he pulled his hand away, there was blood on it. Jaja laughed. Ola had bitten him!

The lord reached to grab her, but Ola skipped away and ran toward the ship's side, where she jumped onto the railing and without hesitating, dove into the water far below. Jaja rushed to the side and looked down.

"Ola! Ola!" he called.

"Jaja! Jaja!" she called back. There was no fear in her eyes now, and as she sank beneath the water, a smile lighted her face like the rising sun turns dark trees green.

"Ola! Ola!"

She resurfaced. Jaja could have sworn she was laughing, and then she disappeared and was seen no more. Before anyone realized it, three other captives had leaped into the water, smiles and laughter lighting their faces like stars.

Quickly the lords pushed and shoved everyone down into the belly of the ship, not caring if they fell down the steps or not. That evening when they were brought back on deck, nets had been stretched outward from the ship so that anyone who jumped would land only in them.

But that did not stop those intent on dying. One morning a few days after Ola became free, the white man who spoke their tongue came to Jaja.

"You! They say you are their leader."

Jaja shook his head. "They are mistaken."

"I don't think so. Come on!"

Jaja was taken to the other end of the ship, where he saw Obasi lying as if dead.

"This one refuses to eat. They say you can make him eat."

Jaja knelt beside his teacher and gently stroked his face. Obasi smiled. They did not exchange any words around this white man who understood their language, but each spoke by putting words directly into the other's mind.

You look very peaceful, my teacher.

I am. I am. Soon I will be where the Lords of the Dead cannot reach me. Why shouldn't I be at peace?

I wish I could join you.

I wish you could too. There is so much I have not told you. But do not worry, Jaja. One day. One day.

Jaja stood up. "His spirit has left him. Among our people, if one's spirit dies, there is no person."

The lord laughed derisively. "Well, where you're going nobody gives a damn about your spirit." He bent over Obasi. "Listen. If you don't eat, I'm going to knock your teeth out and make you eat."

"Just because you force food into me, it does not mean I will live."

"We'll see about that." And without another word, the lord hit Obasi in the mouth as hard as he could. Jaja focused on the Place of Seeing, and as the pain began spreading through Obasi's face, Jaja drew it out and sent it winging onto the wind. Again and again, the white man hit Obasi in the face, and teeth hung loosely from his jaws as blood poured between his lips. But Obasi felt nothing.

You have learned well, Jaja. In peace.

In peace, Master.

Obasi was tossed overboard like a piece of meat that had rotted. Jaja watched as sharks came quickly to the body. Where, one moment there was a human being, the next, there was only blood.

Many days passed without event. Then one morning when they were brought on deck, they saw land in the distance. The lords were very excited and Jaja knew they had spied the faint outlines of whatever place they called home.

He turned to look back across the expanse of sea on the other side of which was the place he called home. He knew now that he would never see it again. Whatever this place was to which the ship was bringing them, it would never be home. No one here would speak his language. No one here would know about the power. No one here would understand.

You can only talk if there is someone who understands. No one in this new place could. Then how could he speak?

III

"Water! Water!"

The Old African awoke immediately. Those were the first words the boy had said in almost three days. The fever had broken. The Old African pulled himself off the floor from beside the bed and made his way unerringly in the darkness to the pail of water by the fireplace. He took the gourd floating in the bucket, filled it with water, and brought it to the boy.

The boy pushed the gourd away. "No. No. Water! Everywhere! Water!" Just as suddenly as he had spoken, he was again asleep.

What is that boy talking about? the Old African wondered. He drank the water he had brought for the boy, and then he remembered something Riley had said. He hadn't paid any attention at the time because he was concentrating on making the boy's heartbeat stronger, but now he recalled Riley saying something about finding the boy at the ocean. Maybe he hadn't paid any attention because it wasn't a word he

recognized. Ocean. What was that? And what did the boy mean just now when he said water everywhere?

He was too tired to think about it now, and he lay back down on the floor. He didn't think he had been asleep long, when he felt someone touch him. He awoke instantly.

"Easy. Easy," came a soft voice.

The Old African relaxed when he recognized May. She was the only one who had never been afraid of him, who came to his cabin in the woods. He wouldn't live in what they called the slave quarters. He was nobody's slave and he refused to live among slaves. They had no memories except those of slavery because they had been born slaves and would die slaves and in between, they would live in little houses and spend their lives saying "Yes, Master" and "No, Master."

But May wasn't like that. Her mouth said "Yes, Master" and "No, Master," but he could tell: Her heart was saying something else. She reminded him of Ola, not that he remembered now what she looked like. But memories also resided in feelings, and that was where he knew May. If he ever spoke again, he thought it might be to her. But after so long, he wondered if he even had a voice anymore. However, he did put his words into May's mind when he wanted to tell her something.

She usually came in from the field with him every evening to help him tend the herb garden he had growing behind his cabin. On Sundays, when they didn't work in the fields, she went through the woods with him, digging roots and collecting bark for the medicines he made up. But she only came and woke him if somebody had taken sick.

"Africa Man. Ol' Riley tol' me to come tell you that you best be in the fields bright and early tomorrow or else you'll be under the field before noontime."

The Old African nodded. The message was not a surprise. However, he was surprised that Riley had told May to tell him instead of coming himself. It wasn't like Riley to use a slave woman to carry his threats. So Riley was afraid of him.

When a man like Riley became afraid, he was as dangerous as a hurt animal.

"Water! Water!" came a soft voice from the bed.

May moved toward the bucket by the stove, but the Old African caught her by the arm, stopping her.

Listen to him. May heard the words in her mind.

She moved to the side of the bed. "You want some water, Paul?" she asked softly.

Paul opened his eyes. "May," he said, and smiled. "May. I saw water, May."

"That's nice."

"No, May. You don't understand. When I ran away from here. I wasn't planning on staying away so long. But on the third day I started to hear this sound and I just had to find out what it was. So I kept walking and then I came to it." He sat up in the bed, his eyes wide, a big smile on his face. "As far as I could see, there was nothing but water. It went all the way to the edge of the world where it touched the sky."

May snorted in disbelief. "What you talking about, Paul? I'd probably see something like that if I took the beating you did."

"No, May. I saw it. That's where I was all this time. I was looking at the water."

The Old African could not believe what he was hearing. That boy had seen the Water-That-Stretched-Forever, and from what he said, it didn't seem to be far from here.

May got up from the bed. "Well, that's real nice, Paul. But I need to get ready to get in the field." Then she looked at the Old African. "I'll tell Ol' Riley you said you'll be in the field with the sun tomorrow."

What was Riley like when he told you to give me those words?

May frowned. "So drunk, he could hardly stand on the porch. He looked meaner than I have ever seen him."

The Old African nodded and he sent his mind into the house where the slave master lived, and there the Old African saw Riley sitting in a chair at his desk, a bottle of whiskey to his left and his pistol to his right. And in Riley's mind the Old African saw himself lying dead on the ground outside his cabin, blood pouring from a bullet wound in his head, Riley standing over him, a drunken grin of triumph on his face. Riley had no intention of letting the Old African get anywhere near the field tomorrow or any other morning.

The Old African glanced at the boy, who was wide-awake now. He would be up and about later that day, and that was good. The Old African was going to need him.

Can you feed the boy before you go to the field? the Old African silently asked May.

"Sure. Where are you going?"

The Old African shook his head and slipped out of his cabin and into the surrounding woods until he came to a large boulder in a clearing. He had come to the boulder often in the first years on the plantation. Its hardness and solidity had been an odd kind of comfort. *I endure,* the boulder told him. *Be still and silent. Do not rage. Do not weep. Do not wish for anything. Be and endure.*

The Old African had learned that enduring was a power too, and just as he had been drawn to the boulder, so the slaves, after a while, were drawn to him. No matter what happened, his emotions never rose or fell. He was there for them like the boulder was there for him.

But this morning the Old African's emotions crashed through his body like the water that rose and fell with the never-ending roar. Ocean. That was the word. What if it was the same as the Water-That-Stretched-Forever? He had to be sure. He had to see for himself.

It had been so long since he had used his power for anything except healing. An important part of his training had been learning to see the world as animals, trees,

insects, and almost anything else did. That was how he knew which plants, roots, and tree barks were good for what ailments and wounds. He heard the whispers of weeds and flowers and leaves. Although he could still speak and listen to a tree or a lizard, he did not know if he still had the power to actually become them.

He wished he had time to practice, to change himself into a stick or a pebble first, just to see if he could still do it. But he had to act quickly. If what he had in mind was going to happen, it had to happen that night. Something had to happen that night because Ol' Riley was intent on killing him by morning.

The Old African closed his eyes and pictured a bird in his mind, a bird with yellow eyes that could look down from the nave of heaven and see a rabbit running, a bird with wings as wide as salvation, a bird with a beak so sharp, it could rip out the heart of a Lord of the Dead, a bird with talons that could grasp sorrow and squeeze the blood from it.

He kept his eyes fixed on the image for a long time, but nothing happened. Finally he opened his eyes and looked around. Perhaps it had been too long. Or maybe he was trying to do too much at once.

He closed his eyes again. This time he thought only of the bird's round yellow eyes. As he did, he felt his own eyes shrink in size. His heart beat faster with excitement as his mind shifted rapidly to the other parts of the bird—its head, wings, legs, talons—and just as rapidly, he felt his head shrink, his arms extend into feathers, his legs tighten, and his feet turn into claws. As he opened his eyes, his wings opened too, and he rose into the air.

His wings beat in broad graceful strokes until he felt a strong undercurrent of wind, and he let his wings rest on the wind as it took him high into the sky. Looking down, he could see the slaves in the field, backs bent, heads down as they hoed at the weeds. To his hawk's eyes May looked as close to him as if she were sitting

across the table eating. He gave a hawk's cry and May raised her eyes.

"Look!" she called, pointing to the hawk wheeling in the sunlight high above them.

The slaves shaded their eyes to stare at the bird. "What you think it feel like to be that free?" Little John, May's brother, asked.

"What would you do if you was free?" May asked him.

"Nothing. That's what being free to me would be like. I could wake up in the morning and do nothing. What would you do?"

"Me? I would be like that hawk there and fly at the sun."

The hawk had no time to listen to their words. Instead its eyes moved restlessly back and forth as it went round and round in a wide circle. Higher and higher it moved on circles of wind, looking, looking, looking. Finally, it thought it saw what it was looking for.

The hawk dropped down to a height where the winds were not as strong and, moving its great wings rapidly, went toward the blue-green color. Before long it was close enough to see it clearly. Yes! That was it! The Water-That-Stretched-Forever!

The hawk flew until it was directly over the ocean. It looked across the expanse of water to the point where water and sky seemed to meet. Somewhere beyond that place was home. Home! Jaja could not believe that he was hearing himself say that word. Home.

Rapidly the hawk flew back from where it had come. This time it did not stop to soar above the slaves working in the field, and when May saw the great bird flash past and then drop from the sky into the woods near the Old African's house, she wondered.

The Old African resumed human form almost immediately after landing on the boulder. How wonderful it had been to be free! He had almost forgotten what it was like to be able to enjoy the warmth of the sun without a care in the world. But perhaps his flight would not have been as sweet if he had not known that he was going home.

There was no time to waste. He had to get May and the other slaves in from the field immediately.

The Old African closed his eyes again. However, this time instead of changing form, he gathered energy from the base of his spine, the place Obasi called the Source of All Power, and brought it slowly up his spinal column, into his neck and head, where it joined the energy of the Place of Seeing. He put his head back and sent the energy through the Place of Seeing and into the sky in a continuous stream. The longer he did so, the greater the energy that poured from him until finally, there, clouds began rolling in from the direction of the Water-That-Stretched-Forever.

But these were not like the ordinary clouds that brought showers. These were tall and black and came in a procession, one after the other. When the slaves in the field saw them, Henry, the oldest slave on the plantation, was the only one who recognized what they looked like. "Slave ships!" he exclaimed in his ancient voice. "Thems is slave ships!"

There looked to be hundreds of them, with lightning dancing through their blackness like whips of fire, and the claps of thunder rattled the dishes in the sideboard in Master Riley's dining room.

"We got to get out of here!" May yelled, and dropping their hoes, the slaves started running toward the quarters.

The clouds continued to roll in from the ocean, darkening the sky. They seemed to be coming from where the ocean slapped the sand on the other side of the world, coming as if they had been waiting for someone to summon them.

Bolts of lightning leaped down from the clouds and hit John Riley's house like rifle shots, breaking windows, splitting doors, singeing rugs until the house itself burst into flames like a flower opening. The thunder rolled back and forth across the sky like applause, and it was so loud, no one heard the screams of John Riley as the flames turned him as black as the hold of a slave ship.

Daniel, the slave preacher, gathered all the slaves in his cabin because he knew this was the Judgment Day he had been asking the Lord for all these years. "I want you to come down, Ol' Maker. Come down this afternoon and make these evil white folks know that they are sinners. Bend their bodies low and make their eyes to weep and set us free like you done the children of Israel back there in the olden days in Egypt."

And while the slaves shouted "Amen!" and sang, May hurried to the cabin of the Old African. When she rushed inside, Paul was dancing around the room, a big grin on his face.

"Can't you feel it, May? Can't you feel it? We free, May! We free!"

"What you talking about, boy?" she responded. "You must still got a fever!"

"No, May! Noooo! Africa Man. He told me."

May looked around for the Old African but didn't see him. "What do you mean, he told you? Did he speak to you?"

Paul frowned. "Well, kind of. He didn't move his lips. In fact, he wasn't even in the room. I ain't seen him all day, but I heard a voice inside my head and it said, 'Your name is now Oji because you brought us a great gift. You have brought us the way to freedom.'"

May shook her head. "I know you crazy now. What kind of name is . . . is . . . whatever you said."

"Oji!" he repeated proudly.

The door of the cabin flew open just as the sky exploded with lightning and thunder from one end to the other and the land shook like it was sobbing with grief. The Old African stepped inside just as the clouds opened and rain came down like rocks. May stepped back at the sight of him. His face looked as if it were being lighted from inside his skull. She had never seen anyone who looked so alive! And then she knew.

"It was you, wasn't it? That hawk up in the sky that was looking down on us this morning. That was you. And this storm what come like God's own vengeance. That's your doing. Ain't it?"

It is time to go home, Bayo!

The Old African was smiling at her. Smiling! She hadn't known he could.

Bayo was my mother's name. It means, in you joy is found.

"Bayo," she repeated.

"Oji," the boy said.

They looked at each other and laughed.

How many slaves want to be free?

Both of them heard the words.

"Everybody!" Bayo said emphatically. "Just because somebody say 'Yes, Mastah,' it don't mean he don't want to be free."

"That's right!" Oji agreed.

Then go. Say to them: All that want to be free should get ready to go.

"But—but we can't go nowhere in all this lightning and thunder and rain you done brought on."

No one will be out looking for runaways in weather like this, will they?

Bayo smiled and nodded her head. "Come on!" She motioned to Oji, and the two ran through the rain to the slave quarters.

IV

Daniel, the slave preacher, was the one who noticed that the rain mysteriously stopped when the sun went down, and that was when the Old African gave the signal for them to move. How could they travel at night when they couldn't see, they wondered that first night, but the Old African seemed like he had the vision of an owl and the sure step of a cat. Then, as day was about to break, the clouds came rushing in and filled the sky, and the rain came down like anger that will never be appeased. The Old African always seemed to find a cave or an old abandoned barn where they could stay dry.

"This is the Lord's doing!" Daniel preached. "The Lord has come down here to help us just like He done the Hebrew children. Don't you see? He's causing it to rain by day so the white folks can't follow us, and we move at night when it's too dark for anyone to find us. Praise the Lord, children! Praise His name!"

But Oji and Bayo knew different. Or thought they did. The Old African was glad for Daniel's preaching. The more the people believed they were being helped by their God, the more easily they would be willing to do what he was asking them to do.

It was midway through their journey on the second night that he heard it. It sounded just as he remembered it, a constant unrelenting sound whose tone never varied in pitch or loudness.

"That's it!" Oji exclaimed. "That's it!"

And as the day began to break, they saw it. The Old African stood at the edge of the woods and looked down a slope and out onto an expanse of water that stretched until it touched the sky.

"This is it!" Oji shouted. "This is it! Ain't it the prettiest thing you've ever seen?"

The slaves nodded and muttered in awed agreement. But then Daniel noticed the orange disc of the sun rising up from the water at the edge of the world. Had the Lord abandoned them by not sending clouds and rain to hide their presence? What were they supposed to do now that they were here? There was nowhere to go!

How many want to go to Africa with me?

The question appeared in all their minds at the same time. They looked at each other. What was the Old African talking about? How were they going to get to Africa? There were no boats there.

Daniel spoke. "I reckon all us *want* to go anywhere that ain't here. But we don't see how we can get there."

The Old African took Bayo by the hand and walked with her down to the water. She squealed as the cold water touched her bare feet, but the Old African continued walking deeper into the water, holding her hand tightly. The water swirled about her ankles and then her knees. When it reached her thighs, she started trying to pull away from him, but he tightened his grip.

Do not be afraid. Trust me.

She was still afraid, but she trusted the Old African just as she trusted rain to be wet. So she relaxed even as the water reached her chest, neck, lips, nose, and then she and the Old African disappeared from sight.

The slaves standing on the shore were stunned. Had that African brought them all that way just so they could watch him kill himself? What kind of sense did that make? And how come he took May with him? Even Daniel didn't know how any of this fit into God's plan. God had parted the waters for Moses and the children of Israel. These waters didn't part an inch. Only Oji seemed like he wasn't bothered, a smile on his face.

The orange disc of the sun rose out of the ocean until it sent its rays in a swatch across the water.

The slaves had begun wondering why they were still standing there. It was time to find someplace to hide until they figured out what to do.

Then Little John exclaimed, "Well, won't you look at that?"

There were May and the Old African walking up out of the water, still holding hands like they had just taken a stroll in the woods. The slaves rushed down to the water's edge to make sure it was them. They gathered around May, touching her arms and shoulders to see if she was really flesh and blood.

"I walked on the bottom of the water just like I was walking across a field. I—I don't know how Africa Man made me do it, but he did. I breathed just as normal as if I was breathing air."

Daniel laughed and then shouted, "I knew the Lord wouldn't desert His children. Thank you, Lord. Thank you! Let's go to Africa, children! I don't know what's in Africa, but I sho' know what's here. I don't know about you, but I believe I'll take a chance on what I don't know rather than to keep on living with what I do."

"Amen! Amen!" everyone shouted.

As the Old African turned and began walking back into the water, the slaves followed him. They squealed and giggled as the cold water first touched them, but as they felt its power against their legs, some became frightened. The Old African sensed the fear immediately.

Breathe deeply. In and out. In and out.

The frightened ones did so and they became calmer.

The Old African led them down to the bottom of the ocean as if there were steps to walk on. The people were surprised that even though they were in water, they did not feel wet or cold, and once on the bottom, they walked like they were on dry land. Fish of every color and size swam around them as if seeing people walking across the ocean floor was something they encountered every day.

Time disappeared, as there was no morning and night in that realm. So the Old African did not know how much time had passed before two sharks glided into view. He felt the people behind him shudder at the sight of the large fish. Though none of them had ever seen one, they knew they were in the presence of killers.

A shark gently nudged the Old African, as if wanting him to change direction. He did so without hesitation, and the two sharks took their places beside him, one on each side, and he let them lead. However, the Old African himself became a little nervous when he began noticing more and more sharks swimming alongside them. He remembered how the sharks had torn Obasi to pieces like he had been dried straw. Were they going to do the same to them?

But the sharks made no move to attack anyone.

Finally the Old African saw ahead of him other sharks swimming back and forth across their path, blocking the way. But as he came closer, they swam aside.

It took a moment for the Old African to understand what he was seeing. There on the ocean floor, as far as he could see, were skeletons, one beside the other, row after row after row, arms by their sides.

Then the Old African heard a voice inside his head.

We are sorry. We were made by the Creator to eat living flesh. We are sorry we ate these and we have tended their bones in hopes that one day someone would come. And now you have.

The Old African could not stop the tears that came into his eyes as he stared at the rows and rows of skeletons. Which one was Ola? Which Obasi? And who were all of these others who were thrown or leaped from the decks of slave ships? So so many. It seemed the skeletons stretched into forever.

Thank you, the Old African told the sharks. *Will you do us a favor?*

We would be happy to.

Please show us the way home.

It is not far.

As the sharks began to swim away and the Old African and the others followed, Oji thought he saw the skeletons move.

"Africa Man!" he called out.

The Old African turned back and to his amazement, the skeletons were rising up and beginning to walk beside them. As far as he could see, behind him skeletons walked as calmly as if they did not know that they were dead. But the sharks did not seem surprised by the procession they were leading.

Soon the Old African felt the bottom of the ocean starting to rise.

Welcome home!

Thank you. Thank you for everything, the Old African told the sharks.

And then, they were gone.

The ocean floor rose higher and higher until suddenly, the Old African's head came out of the water and he walked slowly onto a beach of sand as white as forgiveness. The others followed, amazed that they had walked to Africa.

"Look!" Bayo shouted.

The Old African turned his gaze away from his homeland back to the water, where he saw the skeletons rising out of it. But as they did so, their bodies were returned to them and they walked onto the beach like people who had just taken a swim.

The air was filled with the sound of many languages as husbands and wives hugged each other and there were shouts and laughs of joy as children returned to the arms of their parents.

The Old African looked anxiously now as more emerged from the ocean, but he did not see anyone he knew, did not see the only one he so desperately wanted to see.

Bayo knew by the sadness on his face that he had been hoping to find someone. "I'm sorry," she told him.

The waters were still once more as no one else came up from the ocean. The Old African turned away.

"Wait," Bayo said, touching his arm. "Here come two that almost got left behind."

The Old African turned around and saw a man and a woman, and the woman was as beautifully black as a crow's flight. For the first time since he had last called her name, he opened his mouth and called, "Ola! Ola!"

"Jaja! Jaja!"

He ran down to the water and threw his arms around her and she threw hers around him, and they held each other like the sky holds the sun. Finally, Jaja turned and embraced Obasi. "Master!"

Obasi chuckled. "No. It is you I should address as Master! Look what you have done."

The sand was crowded with all the captured ones who had died or been killed and thrown into the Water-That-Stretched-Forever.

Welcome home.

All of them heard the same thing in their minds. Then Bayo and Oji laughed.

"It's okay to talk now, Africa Man," Bayo told him.

Jaja laughed. Yes, it was. They would understand him.

"Welcome home!" he called out. "Welcome home!"

A NOTE FROM THE AUTHOR

In 1972 I published *Long Journey Home*, a book of stories based on true incidents in black history. The title story was inspired by a legend I found in a then out-of-print book, *Drums and Shadows: Survival Studies Among the Georgia Coastal Negroes*, about a place in Georgia called Ybo Landing where, it was believed, a group of Ybo slaves had walked into the water, saying they were going to walk back to Africa.

After the book was published I received a letter from Jean Levens, an acquaintance from Macon, Georgia, who sent me a local map showing "Ebo Landing." To my surprise it was on a river inlet on St. Simon's Island, Georgia. Why had I imagined Ybo Landing as being on the ocean? But, even after learning that the actual place was not on the ocean, the beach I had seen in my imagination remained unchanged.

From time to time I found myself musing over the story of Ybo Landing. Much of literature stems from the writer asking him- or herself, "What if . . ." wondering: What if those Africans actually did walk from St. Simon's Island all the way back to Africa? How could they have done it?

The answer to the last question came eventually from a source to whom I had made references for a long time in autobiographical writings, a figure I called the Old African. He was not an actual person to me but a symbol for the African and slave aspects of my collective past. But one January day in 1997 he presented himself to me. I was startled to see that his spirit was old but he was young. He was watching a young slave being whipped but the Old African was taking the young slave's pain into himself. If anybody knew how to walk across the bottom of the ocean back to Africa, it was the Old African. I sat down at the computer and wrote the book in three weeks.

The other impetus for this book is the creative partnership I've had with illustrator Jerry Pinkney since 1986. We have sought to create books in which the art and text are inter-dependent and create a whole neither could be alone. From the moment I started writing *The Old African* I knew I wanted Jerry to illustrate it. Thus, I sought to make the language as visually rich as I could, and more so than I might have otherwise. Quite frankly, I was curi-ous to see what Jerry would come up with. He has exceeded anything I could have imagined.

This book is an expression of a creative relationship between two men born eleven months apart, I in January 1939, and Jerry Pinkney in December of that year, and of our relationship and indebtedness to our African ancestors, those who survived that voyage from there to here, and those who did not. In this book we take them home.

A NOTE FROM THE ARTIST

I remember vividly my first reading of *The Old African*, conscious of the possibility that it could be my next illustration project. I was stunned at the power and poetry of its creative language. But it seemed to me that Julius's masterful text was complete in itself. I couldn't help but ask myself, What role could I play?

I called Phyllis Fogelman, my editor and publisher at the time, who told me that Julius had written the legend with me in mind, intending the book to be fully illustrated. And so I set the manuscript aside for a while, hoping that a vision would crystallize in time.

It did—in the memory of an exhibition mounted at the Schomburg Center for Research in Black Culture. The subject was Chattel Slavery from Africa to the Americas. In this exhibit, one bore witness to the brutality of the Black Holocaust. On view were instruments used to shackle and mutilate the body, and the spirit. I had left the exhibit feeling wounded—a feeling similar to the one I'd had upon reading Julius's depictions of the enslavement of the Ybo.

My vision for *The Old African* began to take shape. In my thoughts I began interpreting the text in a way that would focus on Yboland, Nigeria, to speak to the suffering, courage, and triumph of the enslaved Ybos in coastal Georgia.

I returned to the Schomburg Center, and met with Howard Dodson and Sylviane A. Diouf. It was imperative that I learn as much as possible about the Ybo people. Sylviane shared invaluable written material. Most significantly, she gave me the name of an African historian, John Oriji. An Ybo himself, John lives and teaches in the United States. I sent him a list of requests and he graciously responded with written as well as visual references.

With research firmly in place, I was then able to enter the story's pivotal sense of a mythical time and space. In some ways it was that mythological presence that allowed me to paint pictures that were layered with such intense subject matter.

In the process of developing the paintings, I was forced to abandon my usual method of relying on models for expressions and postures. It would be too large a task. I would have to inhabit the characters. I began by sketching, searching for supporting reference, drawing, and redrawing over and over again.

Julius's text was the platform and inspiration for my pictures. His characters formed bonds in spite of their circumstances. The gravity of these family ties became the pulse of my art. John's assistance brought a visual authenticity to my work. Many months of research was the fuel to keep me going, as was my wife, Gloria Jean, who was always at my side, guiding, supporting, and nurturing me throughout this two-year journey.